Zebra Technologies believes in "doing well by doing good" with our customers, partners, and local communities through philanthropy and volunteer activities. Our employees are our company's greatest asset, and our success is based on a strong corporate culture. We are a company built on great minds with diverse points of view that come together as a dynamic community of builders, doers, and problem solvers. Zippy's experience reflects the opportunity we all have to celebrate our differences and create a sense of belonging for everyone. We are excited to share this story with you and shine a light on Bernie's Book Bank and its positive role in supporting young readers.

- Anders Gustafsson
CEO, Zebra Technologies

We appreciate Zebra Technologies' support of Bernie's Book Bank. Our shared vision of promoting literacy for children of all ages and backgrounds makes our world a better place. We are "changing the story" for our children to help them read their way to a better life. Zippy's story reminds us that we each have a purpose, and we can help others achieve significance at the highest level. By connecting books with those who need them, we provide children the ability to learn about life through the characters. We also offer young readers a window into the experiences of others, which is critical to building a foundation for success while also teaching empathy from a young age. Enjoy *Zippy's Special Gift*—it is a gift that keeps giving for all who share it!

- Brian Floriani
Founder, Bernie's Book Bank

This book is dedicated to all of those who love to read and those who make reading possible! Zebra Technologies is proud to support Bernie's Book Bank and its commitment to transforming the educational journey of thousands of children by giving them the tools they need to become successful readers. Profits from the sales of this book will be donated to Bernie's Book Bank to help the organization continue to provide books for a better life!

Visit berniesbookbank.org

www.mascotbooks.com

Zippy's Special Gift

For more information, please contact:
Mascot Books
620 Herndon Parkway, Suite 320
Herndon, VA 20170
info@mascotbooks.com

Library of Congress Control Number: 2020917565

CPSIA Code: PRT1020A
ISBN-13: 978-1-64543-674-4

Printed in the United States

Zippy's
Special Gift

Therese Van Ryne

Illustrated by
Walter Policelli

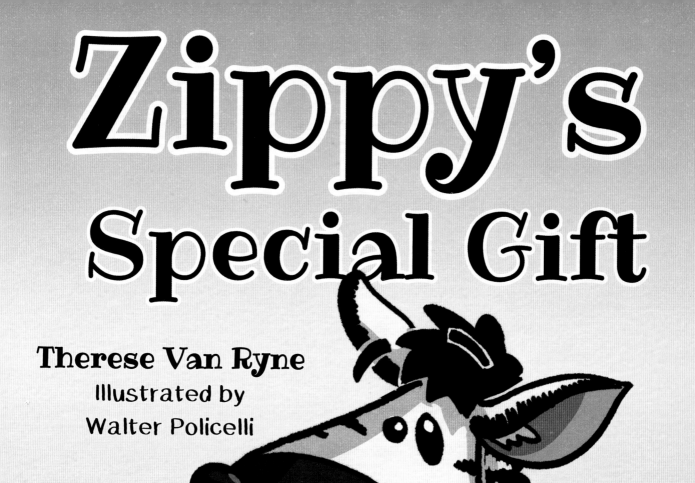

Zippy was a young Zebra who really loved to play.

She also loved to run and jump
and eat the grass all day.

Zippy had so many friends—
like Duck, Owl, and Frog.

Some days, she had a lot of fun
with Monkey and Dog.

One day, Zippy asked her mother,
"Why don't I look like my friends?"

Her mother said, "Your stripes are a special gift that never ever ends!"

"But I don't like them," Zippy said as she put her head down low.

Her mother said, "Now, Zippy, there's something you should know."

"Your friends all have special gifts, too,
and that gives them each their style.

Go ask them, and they'll tell you,"
her mother said with a smile.

"What's your special gift?"
Zippy asked Duck as the sun
started to dim.

Duck said, "Though I don't like the looks of them, my webbed feet sure help me swim!"

When Zippy asked Owl about his gift,
he replied, "I can hoot!

I don't always like the sound I make, but it's better than toot, toot!"

Frog was next on Zippy's list, if she
didn't go too deep.

"While some days I wish I could walk like
you, my special gift is my leap!"

As Zippy continued on her journey, she started to notice a trend.

Though it may not be their favorite thing, a gift was bestowed on each friend.

Up next was Zippy's friend, Monkey, who was hanging from a tree.

He said, "It gets in the way sometimes,

but my tail is a special gift to me!"

Finally, Zippy found her friend, Dog,
who was in flowers as she sniffed.

"My nose is always so busy," said Dog.
"My sense of smell is my gift!"

"You're right!" Zippy said to her mother when she returned to their home.

"Now I know why I have my stripes,"
Zippy said as her voice rang true.

"These stripes are my special gift because they make me look like you!"

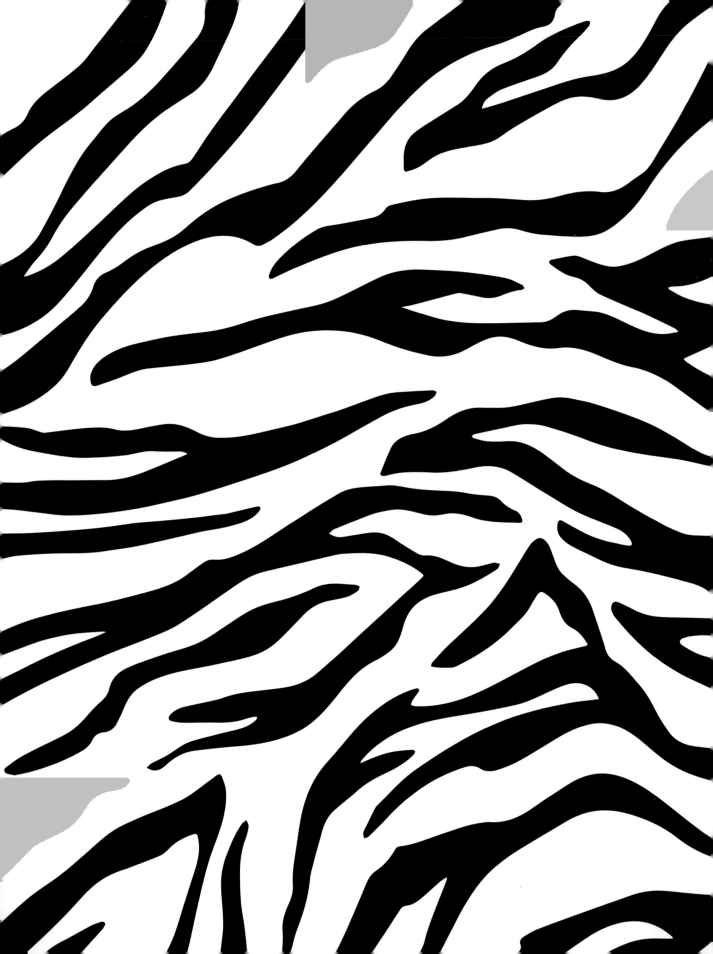

Zippy Comes to Life

For over 50 years, Zebra Technologies has helped people around the world with solutions to keep them connected and make better business decisions. Zippy the Zebra is our mascot, representing our diverse culture and the fun we like to have at work. In this book, Zippy introduces us to her connections—her best animal friends who help her make an important decision about herself.

Visit zebra.com

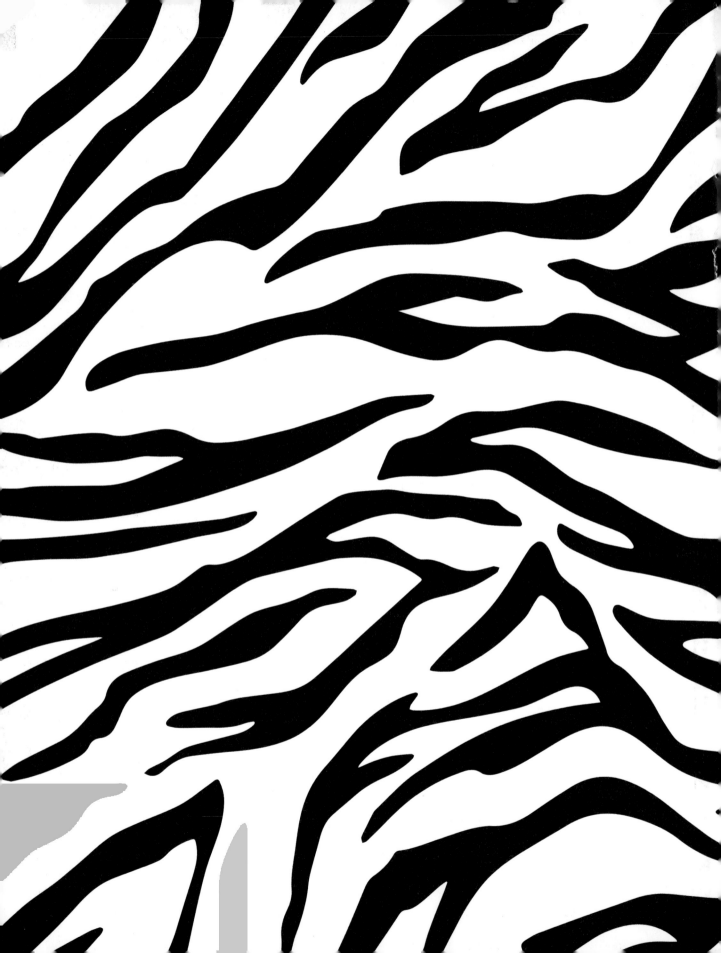